Dedicated to my mother

HarperCollins
PUBLISHERS
Since 1817

Toad on the Road   Copyright © 2017 by Stephen Shaskan   All rights reserved. Manufactured in China.   No part of this book may be used or reproduced in any manner whatsoever without written permission except in the case of brief quotations embodied in critical articles and reviews. For information address HarperCollins Children's Books, a division of HarperCollins Publishers, 195 Broadway, New York, NY 10007.   www.harpercollinschildrens.com   ISBN 978-0-06-239347-0   The artist used Photoshop to create the digital illustrations for this book.   Typography by Rachel Zegar   17 18 19 20 21 SCP 10 9 8 7 6 5 4 3 2 1   ❖   First Edition

STEPHEN SHASKAN

TOAD
on the
ROAD

A Cautionary Tale

HARPER
An Imprint of HarperCollinsPublishers

Toad on the road.
Toad on the road.
Oh no! Oh no!
There's a toad on the road!

Who's that coming down the road?
Oh yikes! Oh yikes!
It's a . . .

Bear on a bike!

Everyone shout:
Look out! Look out!

Hey, little toad, get out of the way!
You could get hurt. That's no place to play.

Vamoose! Skedaddle! Without delay!
What do you think your mama would say?

Toad on the road.
Toad on the road.
Oh no! Oh no!
There's a toad on the road!

Who's that coming down the road?
My stars! My stars!
It's a . . .

Croc in a car!

Everyone shout:
Look out! Look out!

Hey, little toad, get out of the way!
You could get hurt. That's no place to play.

Vamoose! Skedaddle! Without delay!
What do you think your mama would say?

Toad on the road.
Toad on the road.
Oh no! Oh no!
There's a toad on the road!

Who's that coming down the road?
Oh man! Oh man!
It's a . . .

Vole in a van!

Everyone shout:
Look out! Look out!

Hey, little toad, get out of the way!
You could get hurt. That's no place to play.

Vamoose! Skedaddle! Without delay!
What do you think your mama would say?

Toad on the road.
Toad on the road.
Oh no! Oh no!
There's a toad on the road!

Who's that coming down the road?
Good luck! Good luck!
It's a . . .

Toad in a truck!

And what does she say?
Hey, little love, get out of the way!
You could get hurt. That's no place to play.

Vamoose! Skedaddle! without delay!

And that is what your mama would say.